## About the Author

D. Joan is a young writer who grew up writing out her emotions from rough situations. Though she struggled with these situations she became a fine young woman who wanted to be a film editor and director. She wished to give back to the world and create movies that made kids believe in themselves and helped them have hope for a better day than yesterday.

# Miscellaneous Stories

# D. Joan

## Miscellaneous Stories

Olympia Publishers
*London*

www.olympiapublishers.com
OLYMPIA PAPERBACK EDITION

Copyright © D. Joan 2023

The right of D. Joan to be identified as author of
this work has been asserted in accordance with sections 77 and 78 of
the Copyright, Designs and Patents Act 1988.

**All Rights Reserved**

No reproduction, copy or transmission of this publication
may be made without written permission.
No paragraph of this publication may be reproduced,
copied or transmitted save with the written permission of the publisher,
or in accordance with the provisions
of the Copyright Act 1956 (as amended).

Any person who commits any unauthorized act in relation to
this publication may be liable to criminal
prosecution and civil claims for damage.

A CIP catalogue record for this title is
available from the British Library.

ISBN: 978-1-80074-746-3

This is a work of fiction.
Names, characters, places and incidents originate from the writer's
imagination. Any resemblance to actual persons, living or dead, is
purely coincidental.

First Published in 2023

Olympia Publishers
Tallis House
2 Tallis Street
London
EC4Y 0AB

Printed in Great Britain

## Dedication

To all the owners of this book, thank you for picking this book up and reading something that contains pieces of my life. Hopefully you find something in here that resonates with you and helps you realize that you are not alone in your struggle in the world.

# Acknowledgements

You are given a pen, paper, a backpack, pocket money if lucky enough, and a slap on the back when going out into the world. They try to tell you what the world is and what it's not but hell to me could be heaven to you and vice versa. So I thank the pen and paper I was given that helped me through the hard times, I thank God that he showed me the sun when the clouds wouldn't separate, I thank my friends for being there during my high school years and helping me realize that not everyone in this life is as cruel as the others.

Do not forget the people along the way that helped you through your tough times, and don't forget the skills that you possess. Because you never know when they will come in handy in the nearby future. Forgive but don't forget those who have harmed you, a lesson forgotten is a lesson untaught.

# 1

## LOVE'S CONNECTION

What is love but connection, a safe form of surgery between two hearts? Blood flowing from body to body while they love each other longingly and the beating of their hearts, in sync. You laugh, you cry and maybe even fight together. But after it all, you still seem to gravitate toward one another, holding hands in the silence when you have no words for how you feel.

Some hearts stay carefully sewn together for all time. Unfortunately, others have to remember how to beat on their own, their companion ripped from their grasp and the slow burn and filling of sadness knowing that it wasn't forever. You forget how to breathe at that moment, forget how to live in that moment, and feel like it's easier to wither away at that moment. The stitches have been ripped violently only to be summarized, with one word, heartbreak.

# 2

## FIGHTING IN A COLORLESS WORLD

We march and march throughout the streets.

Parading our wants and needs from the amendments in which we hold no place.

We scream but it's as if the city lay bare, without a soul or an ear to listen.

There is no 'I,' there is only 'we.'

Because we are what makes up change.

We are Harriet Tubman, Malcolm X, Martin Luther King Jr., Amanda Gorman, and all the colored influencers in our history.

We are our history, our black history.

You have us singing 'praise the Lord' and taking the N-word into our vocabulary because you're afraid of what might happen if we had diversity and identity.

We would sing and sing together to show that nothing could phase us even if tears were shed.

We ran away so we could have a better life and be treated as normal.

We relied on people like John Brown and events such as the civil war to feel cared for.

But yet all men are created equal.

To this day one hard truth is evident.

While all lives get their rights, black lives have to make them.

# 3

## DARKEST PART OF THE MIND

Have I always been lonely? Besides the knives dancing in and out of my life?
  Yes, very much so.
  But tossing and turning in my mind, I have never been lonely here.
  But the company is unwanted. The company is too much, again, and again haunted by the same story over and over.
  I scream, "Open your eyes."
  A dark classroom, again.
  "Open your eyes."
  A dark shadow, skinny and frightening, again.
  "OPEN YOUR EYES."
  Opened, to a dark abyss, so cold and harsh like the winter.
  Alone again, alone again.

# 4

## CIRCUS OF THE NIGHT

The clown laid lifelessly against the bed frame, his arms limp by his side as his cold smile curled toward the sky. No one ever really slept in this room let alone stood in it for more than a second, but all beds were filled with warm bodies, leaving this one cold and alone.

I sat on the edge of the bed, somewhat hoping that he would disappear, hoping that he was just a dream in my wondrous mind but instead he stood in his exact place. Mocking my genius, mocking my fear that I wish stayed in the pits of my stomach. His face was pale, only darkened circles for eyes, bleeding makeup for tears and a bloody smile for happiness. But everyone knew he wasn't alive, right?

Nearing twelve, I laid back on the dusty bed, and tried my best to ignore the feeling of his hand on my cheek, but the flowing curtains didn't help. They simulated his breath, inching closer and closer to my exposed neck, my exposed skin.

# 5

## HARVEST

That's some strange fruit on that tree.
    It has arms, legs, and a face.
    Its branch ain't made out of wood.
    The fruit is held by its neck.
    It wiggles without the wind to help it along.
    But then it lies still as if the wind has gone.
    With closer inspection you notice a relation between the two.
    We are both human, who knew.

# 6

## DEEP BLUE SEA

Drowning.

Your lungs filled with air but with every gasping breath more and more turns to water. Nothing but bubbles rising in the deep blue. As you grasp at your last chance of life someone breaks the water, pulling you to their boat.

Safety.

Their eyes filled with worry as they wrap a towel around you. Warming you, chasing away the cold as they ask you questions. You stare at them blankly. "What if they're the ones that pushed you?"

Stop it.

"They just have a different face so you can trust them."

Stop…

"They'll probably push you right back in."

That's not true.

"Holding you down till your lungs burn, searching for air."

STOP!

Muffled screams echo in the dark. You open your eyes, feeling your heart racing. Feeling your lungs burning.

You're drowning again.

# 7

## WILTING ROSE PETALS

Roses grow up and out toward the sky.

Their leafy hands touch the sun as the rays grace each petal with its warm glow.

Dew collects on the slick surface, only to slip down onto the rose's neck. Kissing it softly.

"Look, Mommy, a rose!" the child says, plucking the rose from its home and tucking it into his pocket.

Its muscles are sore and tender, missing its lifeline, still rooted in the ground from which it once grew.

"Daddy, Daddy! I picked you a rose."

He handed it to his father, allowing his big hands to cradle it, his fingers to touch the silk and his eyes to simulate the sun.

"It's beautiful, but you hurt this rose, Jacob."

"I did?"

He nodded. "Without its roots it can no longer take from the earth what it needs to survive, and it is now shaded from the sun. And because of that, it shall die."

Grabbing a vase of water, he placed the rose gently inside, setting it by the window. But the child's father had predicted the poor rose's fate.

And day after day its petals turned to rust, curling inward as if shielding itself from the world. Its plump body dried and weakened, forcing its head to rest on the edge.

Its bones aching as the wind brushed against it.

The very nature from which it grew now turned on the wilting husk, tearing it apart, and laying its blackened skin by the windowsill.

The sweet smell of her perfume lessened to nothingness. And all that remained was the shell of the rose, the memory of the summer's end.

# 8

## WRITER'S BLOCK

It's hard having nothing to write about. Your pen is dormant in your hand as you search your mind for something useful and meaningful. You find yourself picking at your skin or staring at the black spot on the ceiling, hoping that it could spell out a topic or even a starting sentence. Time and time again you find a wall, and yet no matter how far you walk or whatever direction you take, you still see it, stretching for miles. This is the great wall, the wall that holds ideas from you, every writer's pain, making it hard to fill your paper with meaningful words rather than the run on sentences about something you barely know. This monstrosity has lived for years, never aging and never dying, we call this, writer's block.

# 9

## DREAMS ARE MADE OF YOU

Dream after dream I see you.

Your pale-white skin glows and your dark brown eyes stare at me, like as if we're here together, like as if we can touch each other again.

But this dream is different, I can feel it.

This time there is no panic, there is no anxiety, there is no longing for me or you, there's peace, calm, and quiet.

You smile for the first time in years, because you found someone who can take care of you like I did, or better than.

The pain you felt is gone and with that smile so is mine, because you solved a problem that I couldn't solve without you.

You helped me see that what happened that night, between us, is over and that we can move on, we can be happy.

Hand in hand with the girl that claims your heart and you smile at me, telling me that you're okay and I love that.

I wake up, smiling to myself because even if I may never see you again, I know you're okay.

– Love you always

# 10

## THE SWEET BIRDIES' CAGE

Metal rattled downstairs behind a big brown door, the cool air sliding under it and in-between your toes as you gripped the handle and waited patiently for the rattling to stop. As it began to slow you opened the door, the air rushed at you and made your hair rise on the back of your neck. You looked to see three cages: one gold, one silver and one bronze – all with different breeds of birds inside. They huddled together tightly as the wind from the wide-open window moved their cages ever so slightly. You approached the cages as the pretty creatures turned to look at you, their heads tilting as you creeped closer.

Once in front of the cages the birds began to chirp in a low whisper as if talking amongst themselves; but as you leaned in, they stopped, copying your movements. You clutched your blanket tightly in one hand as you traced the keyhole on the golden cage with the other. As if reading your mind the birds chirped again, louder and louder, till all you could hear was their voices screaming at you, "Let us out, let us out, LET US OUT!" You looked around for a key but before you could move someone grabbed your shoulder; allowing a small yelp to escape your lips, you turned to see a large, black, featureless figure looming over you as you trembled.

"Don't listen, my darling," the shadow whispered in a raspy voice as it motioned you toward the door. "If they're out there, they can be in harm's way, now you wouldn't want that…" It tilted its head slowly, its neck cracking with every movement. "Would you?" You shook your head frantically as you walked away from the cages; the birds getting quiet again, returning the house to its silent state.

The shadow smiled slightly. "Good." It walked out into the hallway as you slowly followed suit. You looked back to see the birds facing the window and huddling again, as a small blue feather glided in the air and onto the floor; a testament to their pain in the small little cage they called home.

# 11

## RATED M FOR MONSTER

The world seemed forgiving this afternoon, the trees swayed in the wind as the orange, yellow, and red leaves fell like tears at my feet. Several cars ran past me as I walked to the cemetery to say hello to someone 'truly' missed. It's been a while since I saw him that night, it was cold as he faded from his life into his death, his eyes dulling, full of tears as he looked at me, but with people watching me I must act normal like I cared for that moment. When I shoved the knife through his heart.

Dear Dillion, you were like a flower in full bloom that died by my hand. – Mom

The rusted iron gate screamed in agony as I pushed it open. The only thing that made this hell hole lively was the colorful flowers and the wind dancing with the barren trees overhead. I walked with urgency, not giving a damn for the sleeping, decaying bodies underneath my feet. Occasionally I would look around, searching for someone, anyone out of the norm around here. "This is a bunch of bull," I whispered as I walked in front of the grave of my unfortunate choice. I placed the flowers down with paining care as my eyes outlined the engraved words on the hunk of rock in front of me.

'Here lies a beloved friend, boyfriend, and son. 2002–2020' I wonder who spent their time writing this. I rolled my eyes and sat down. *If I'm forced to be here, I should at least act sad and pray or something.*

Dear Dillion, you were like a light in my life which I punched out with ease. – Mom

I walked into my apartment that has been abandoned for years. Cobwebs growing with intensity from when I left until now. Everything was the same, just knocked over or misplaced from when they searched the place. I sighed and began to clean. "Guess no one decided to throw me a welcome back party." After I finished the sun was setting with haste as if it had somewhere to be and I was craving for something other than day-old bread and discolored mac and cheese. I called up a pizza place and they delivered in under thirty minutes, which meant I didn't exactly get a free pizza for my hard labor around the house, but I didn't mind. I laid down on the couch and woke up the TV, after a slice or two, I fell asleep with the TV blaring and the remote nowhere to be found. An unexpected alarm sounded from the black screen of my phone. It had been an a while since I had one in my possession and turning it off was like putting together a five-hundred-piece puzzle with the picture on both the box and puzzle pieces covered. After I had put it to rest, I cleaned up and went to change, being active was part of the contract and I couldn't disobey. I threw on some sweats, running shoes, a headband, and a t-shirt and headed out for a run.

Dear Dillion, you were like a book that held my interest but that burned in my flames – Mom

My legs began to weigh more and more the longer I ran, sweat pouring like water down my face and sticking to my clothes like candy and it didn't help either that it was eighty degrees outside, or that I was wearing a sweater on top of all this rubbish. After thirty more minutes of agonizing pain, I slowed down and walked into the supermarket. Everyone's eyes trailed me as I walked toward the freezer aisle looking for something to put out the fire in my lungs. The freezer was cold making my skin bumpy, and my hair stand on end. It was better than the glass melting heat, but I knew I couldn't stand there forever. I grabbed a soda and ringed it up but before I could even get my wallet out, someone tapped my shoulder. "Excuse me." It sounded like they were in a hurry, so I moved to the side and continued to pay for my savior in a can.

"Thanks," I mumbled and walked out.

"Wait, you dropped something!" a voice cried out. I turned to see it was a woman; she was not that tall but not short either, her hair was black and long, bouncing on her shoulders as she ran my way. She wasn't that thin, and her chest was two steps ahead of her, I couldn't make out her face from the distance but as she got closer, I realized who it was. "Shit."

Dear Dillion, just like you, your old life should be buried, why does it still live to haunt me? – Mom

# 12

## THE BOX

Sitting in a small corner was a box, sometimes my mother would sit on it to tell me and my sister stories when the night was just too scary to bear on our own and other times it would hold our night light that would flicker like a campfire due to the dying battery within. But as always, I'd find myself staring at the box while I waited for Sandman to make it to the lower part of the bunk bed and put me to sleep. I don't know what it was about the box, but it called to me, of course father wouldn't let us near it – let alone open said box under any circumstances. It was like a gift under the Christmas tree, but your parents warned you not to touch it till Christmas day even if you were dying to do so. But, unfortunately, Christmas never came for me, I never got to see what was in the box, never got to touch or shake the box, never even got to inch toward it; after a long silence in the dimly lit room, I yawned and turned away from the box, slowly closing my eyes. Even if I couldn't see what was within the box, I had a strange feeling it could see me…

# 13

## WAITING ROOM

You sat beside a stranger in an all-white room, nothing but chairs and a motivational poster with a cat hanging from a tree that read, 'Hang in there.' But as you continuously darted your eyes from the poster to your smartwatch, you couldn't help but feel the fear that the cat had lacked. You felt as if the cat had mocked your state of emergency and you finally looked at the big iron doors that rested in front of you, you had no clue what lived and thrived beyond those doors but any movement toward it would signal 'Debby S. Jones,' the front desk lady, to give you a stern look while she asked you to sit back down. You mumbled something under your breath as you tapped your foot on the ground, the echoes of your presence startling Debby while she typed God knows what into the computer, probably complaining about your constant need to pace, or tap your foot, or check your watch, even about the disgusted look you gave the poor poster only trying to do its job. But as you finally sat back in your chair the screams of a woman rang out from behind the door, you sprang up and as you tried to walk toward the door the stranger grabbed your hand, you looked toward him as he shook his head, signaling you to sit down.

"This your first time?" he said in a mellow tone, not taking his eyes off his newspaper.

"Y-y-yes."

He chuckled a bit. "She can't deliver the baby if you barge in there, just hang on, it'll be worth the wait." He put down the newspaper as you nodded, tapping your foot rapidly again. "Let me get you a cup of coffee and something to eat, you're gonna need it." He bounced up from his seat and walked off, stuffing his hands in his pockets and making the room just a little bit more peaceful. You sat back in your chair, hoping that you could steal the absence of fear from the kind man.

# 14

## WONDER LAND

Something new and something strange, but it's not all the same.

Tables become chairs, and ceilings become floors in this world of the strange and wondrous. I have no idea where I might have gone but, then again, somewhere is nowhere, and elsewhere is everywhere. Tea parties are a must-have, and cake is every day that isn't your birthday. The smell of love is in the air, or just the smell of freshly painted flowers.

Despite the wonderful and upside-down land, I wish to call home, the people within it are even stranger, from cats who smile in the shadows to caterpillars that fly through the air through the smoke it breathes. But something is wrong, in the distance, a woman yells and yells, making the air burn and my eyes water. Run, little white rabbit, run, hurry, hurry, hurry, down the hole. Before it's off with your head, and, oh, how your head will roll!

Further.
Down.
The hole.
Out of this,
WoNdErLaNd.

# 15

## ILLUSION

Walking around in the park and watching people laugh and play in the sun makes the fall evening a little warmer, when – though you like the cold breeze – a little warmth does feel nice against your skin. As always you smile at their joy and walk off to the café where your friends enjoy some coffee and a little bit of gossip from time to time. They meet your eyes and knowing that there's no escape you sit down and chat with them even if the conversation carries on without you.

    As the sun sets, you say goodbye to your friends and feel a little tug on your heart as the gap between you and them grows wider. Somewhat longing to tell them, "Wait, I still want to hang out and talk," but not wanting to bother them with your issues you keep moving. You get to your house and the second you close the door you press against it, letting your feet drag in front of you and your body slide to the floor.

    The darkness creeps in, replacing the sun and in its place a dark, cold feeling that makes your skin crawl. You reluctantly get up and walk to the bathroom, looking at your face in the mirror you sigh and take off your mask. "Nothing but tear stains and dark circles under your eyes…" you mumble, putting your mask on the bathroom sink. As you walk off to bed, you rub your arms softly, wincing a bit. "Nobody needs to know."

# 16

## STANDSTILL

As the cars come to a stop and people aren't to be seen on either side of the road, it feels as though the world has come to a stop, with only your noise as evidence of life on earth. You ride around on your scooter in the school yard as the world is still on pause, the only thing that lives with you is the insects wisping around and the wind dancing in the trees. But it doesn't last long as one after the other, cars pass by, pressing play on the world; it's not very often the world stops but at least you were there to see the world at a standstill.

# 17

## IMAGINARY FRIENDS

It looks so nice outside today. The sun is shining, and the breeze is relaxing, making your room cool. You hear cars in the distance and hear people talking as they pass by. You sit inside watching whatever show Nickelodeon has provided for today at two o'clock in the afternoon; no one is home at the moment. Mom is at work and Dad is probably somewhere wandering the streets looking for a good place to get drunk. It's only you here, it has always been only you; but sometimes you feel as though there is someone else with you. You can't see them but nonetheless they are there, watching over you, caring for you, laughing and playing with you when you want to waste time.

If only you knew who it was or even what it was. Maybe a nice little friend or one of your plush animals brought to life by your imagination. Who cares really, the only part that really matters is that you have someone to be there when they are not.

# 18

## IT'S JUST A CIGARETTE

The sun creeped into the kitchen, surprising the young woman while she worked on breakfast. Though only a mere week without nicotine in her system she longed for another cigarette from the store underneath the apartment. Her husband sat at the table, opening up the newspaper and humming along to the music on the radio.

She broke shells on the table, placing the perfect yolks into a new, white bowl. The bowl bore art from overseas, making it stand out from the rest in the cabinet. Though small it fit the large eggs nicely as she stirred away, smiling at the results.

As the eggs cooked, she sat near her husband, talking about the latest fridges coming out this Sunday, wondering if they'll add it to the new space. They talked for a minute before she placed the bowl in front of him, his eggs fresh from the stove and ready to eat. She bugged him about a pack of cigarettes as well, his face red, hoping the neighbors were snug in their beds. Knowing it was frowned upon to talk so openly about smoking, especially as a woman of her stature.

After more pleading he agreed, she smiled and kissed him before gracefully going downstairs. She slid the lock from the handle and walked right in, searching for where he stored the cigarettes. Moments passed as she felt for it, a box poking out, surprising her in the dark aisle. She slipped it out and unwrapped it, opening the lid slowly. Smiling, she wiggled one out and got her lighter. Wondering if she could make it last longer than usual, she lit the end, massaging it with the flame until it glowed like a small sun, full of light and promise.

    She wrapped her lips around it and smoked silently in the dark, allowing the smoke to grace her face and play in her hair. Soon after she watched the cigarette slowly disappear, leaving nothing but ashes on the floor. "What a waste," she said as she looked back up. "I should have bought an ashtray."

# 19

## SHIP DOWN SOUTH

***Day One: Boarding the Ship***

It's boarding day, I've got a crate full of supplies for our trip, nothing too much but also nothing too little just in case. My crew have also brought crates of their own, mostly full of beers and games for when we tire of our adventure into the vast seas. The sun is barely out but it's better this way, so we can sail longer in the sun.

***A Few Hours Later***

We've been on the water for a while now, same thing everywhere you look, really… Just water, miles and miles of water. The forecast for today is wonderful, nothing but clear skies and warm weather… As warm as weather gets around water, I suppose, but something is off to me. Can't they feel it? The churning in their stomachs about today, this trip, the water… Something's wrong… I know it.

***Night Time***

It's time to turn in for the night, my bed is near the window that the water gently touches every so often; it is quiet despite the snores and movement from the inside… The water looks calm, and the moon reflects wonderfully on the moving body of water... Sometimes, I wonder if I'd sleep better in a boat house than one on land... But if you're on the water long enough, you take the waves with you – but only for so long. I'm tired but also scared to close my eyes... The lights turn off on deck... You hear that... Waves.

# 20

## JOY'S NOT HERE

Learning is the one thing that never stops, yet so many try to stop it because some believe ignorance is bliss. I believe the opposite but yet learning something today brought about that saying into my mind and tears to my eyes. Even though they didn't grace my face till they free fell to the ground, it still was there – that fear of truth. Some time ago, a couple of months maybe, I felt some type of chill. Not something you feel when you wake up in the dark or in an abandoned house with the faint smell of what could have been lunch. But the chill of joy, some completeness in your life that was never there, and I smiled, because I thought for a moment that this would be something good for me. But, of course, this joy came with weight, and a while after taking hold of this joy I heard of this weight and wanted to let go. I was afraid of stealing this joy from its original owner, yet I never wanted to let go because I felt safe in it, felt as though I could wrap up inside it and sprout something that never was, sprout a small leaf that could turn into something wonderful. That's what I thought this joy could do.

This weight never had a name or face, yet it would come up softly from time to time, as in to shock me and make me drop this joy I denied dropping for months. Never an answer but a simple name when huddling in this joy comes to mind. But like the wind on a hot day, it comes and goes. This joy is mine again.

I develop this love for it, so much so I believe this is some type of faith, some type of destiny, if you will. Hearing it and seeing this joy makes me smile still as strongly as I did when I first got it. But days and maybe weeks go by when this joy is testing the waters, as if wondering if I should even be holding it too. Again, and again left to the blazing sun or the blistering cold as I wait for it, tears that hold my pain fall, and yet, I see it and forget about this pain. I see my joy again.

This joy with a strong sense of playing around does just that, plays with my heart even when it means not, but some part of me believed it knew. And again, like any other time the joy engulfed me, and I felt safe again, the same pattern only this time some weight still clung to its heels, still making me nervous but yet still bold enough to try. Inching toward this joy day by day and just seeing how happy it is, how happy I am, how can this be wrong? Right?

But this thing has an owner, and the owner has glass-filled eyes you might imagine, every time it feels something tugging at their smile, reaching for their bliss, and summoning their laughter throughout the days of it being alone. This owner would feel the poking within their heart knowing that someone was trying to steal their joy. So, I leave it at the table and walk out the door, because it was never mine to begin with, nor was it my house that I stepped in.

# 21

## GONE

The forest lay still as I sped by its trees, overwhelming me turn after turn. Its roots were trying to stop me, trying to catch me. For some reason it was quiet, but not quite enough. I could still hear my footsteps slamming against the cold, somewhat-solid ground, I could hear my erratic breath and I could hear my heart banging in my chest, trying to keep pace. But only faintly, as though I was on another plane – but still in control. I could feel my lungs burning, feel someone shoveling coal into this meat-based existence to keep it warm, keep it alive. But it didn't matter, my legs had a mind of their own and they were taking me far, far, away from I don't know what.

After a few more minutes of absent movement I stopped, gaining consensus slowly and falling to the ground, coughing and reeling in the cool air, putting out the fire inside me. I looked around me, the trees waking up slowly to music I couldn't hear from where I sat. The small patches of grass grazing my legs, bees buzzing around the flowers, and vice versa. What stood out the most was the big white door in front of me, somewhat mocking the nature around it as it stood untouched from the wear and tear, as if someone had recently placed it there. It called to me, the wind pushing me toward it slowly till my hand rested on the cold knob. I twisted it, but it didn't budge. Again. Nothing. But another time and rust falls from the hinges. With much agony the door swings open with a painful cry, but nothing. I close and open the door again to reach the same results; empty space with nothing but white walls, ceilings and floors, somewhat peaceful, somewhat calm. I step in, waiting for the floor to fall under me but it lays sturdy, last thing I hear is the door closing. The last thing I hear is my heart stopping.

Nurses and doctors crowded around his body as they screamed numbers and some type of code. I panicked; my son – my blood, my tears, my joy – was dying, and I couldn't do anything to stop it. The heart monitor raced rapidly before falling, droning on with the same antagonizing noise as the medics pressed on his chest, he was flat lining. "My son," I whispered as they backed away, somewhat afraid of his lifeless body, but it seemed to glow, seemed to harbor his every last breath, just for me. I kissed his forehead, putting my hand on his warm chest, mumbling, "Rest now," as I put the blanket over his face, something warm clung to my chest as I walked out the door and into the parking lot, following me to my car and on the road back home. As I reached my door, it disappeared; David used his last moments to walk me home.

# 22

## UNINVITED

As you lay in bed, you stare at the moon. Listening to the wind as it wrestles with the trees in the dark, somewhat-quiet world. You keep your limbs under your heavy blankets because it seems that they're the only ones that carry warmth amongst the room of ice in which you reside. Here and there you hear stirring throughout the house, knowing that you're alone, you brush it off as just the floorboards, asking for your attention. A little more into the night, the trees quiet down and you begin to drift off, covering your head ever so slightly with your blankets and listening to the silence. The more you allow sleep to take over, you feel calm, but as soon as you fall unconscious your ears catch something – breathing. It seems a guest has arrived unexpectedly, and the party has just begun.

# 23

## ISLAND

Birds chased the wind in the endless sky; they sang, filling the streets with music allowing citizens to dance to work formally as they often did.

Busy bees flooded the streets, knowing that today was no ordinary day. Today something special was found far out west in the depths of the unknown.

*It isn't too much but it's all I need.* "You'll want something bigger."

*I don't.*

"You'll want something richer."

*It provides plenty.*

"You'll want something that everyone can't touch but knows how to form it in their mind. Something everyone wants."

*I have all I need.*

Out in the middle of nowhere, where the tides carried birds and glistening waves to my shores. Truly this was perfect, it was my perfect love. I didn't want to smother it and make it something it wasn't because the flowers and unique trees all sang the sweet song of originality to me. If I change it now, I'll never find it again, for it will blend in with the rest.

I don't want to build on it yet, that comes later. I just

want to enjoy the sand in my hair and the glow on my skin. I want to enjoy all that it brings.

After all this time on a boat in the vast seas, thinking I'll be met with mass defeat.

But no, it's something more greater than that, something grander than life.

I've found where I belong.

I've found my island.

# 24

# THE MAN BEHIND THE LANTERNS' LIGHT

You lean against a wall and slide onto the cold, wooden floor. Nothing but howling wind, and the light of the moon to keep you company in this dark hallway, but then again, the doors are there too. They mock you silently, their golden noses awaiting a slight twist so then it can open to a whole new space, but that slight twist turns into a jiggle, then a frustrated knock, ending with a bang.

Again, you reach for the lamp's string and tug slowly, hearing the echoing click through the hall, but nothing. "The light's out," you mumble once more as you give it another go. Another click echoes before you allow your hand to slip back down to your side. Whimpering in the silence your watery eyes catch a glimpse of a passing light underneath one of the doors. You jump up, "Hello?" it stops, expanding its light toward your cold feet.

You run toward the door and smile for a bit. "Thank God, please you got to help me, the doors won't open, and I've been here for days." And with every word, more and more excitement leaps out; you are finally going to see the last of this hallway, you're finally going to get to see some light. With a small turn of the knob from the other side, you put your hand on the knob and turn with it, the lock clicks. "Yes, yes, yes!"

Flinging the door open you run toward the light. It seems farther than before, but you don't care. Your feet feel the warm embrace of the carpet beneath you, and the warm heat from the heaters on either side of the darkened space. Closer and closer, brighter and brighter, just a little more before your eyes are blinded by the heavenly lights. So consumed by the hope, the escape, you fall to your knees and cry tears of joy; finally, you're out.

You open your eyes, having your heart fall down into the crevasse of your chest. These tears of joy suddenly turn into tears of pain, and your hands touch the cold floor. "No, no, please! Please!" You run to the door and bang against it till your hands turn sore. This shouldn't be happening, but it is. You're back where you started. You're back in the darkened hallway again.

Like clockwork, you lean against the barren wall, feeling the floor's cold embrace as you stare off into the night. Your hand reaches for the lamp and tugs on its string once more, but instead of being left in the moonlight, the room lights up from the snapping of its fingers. This is new. This is different. Like a child experiencing something new, you stare at the smiling lamp with wonder. Something different has happened, all because of the light underneath the door.

Sitting up, you smile to yourself and look at the oak door in anticipation. Because you have a feeling, the light will walk past again. Again, you will wait for the man behind the lanterns' light.

# 25

## OLD HABITS DIE HARD

You've come home, how fun… But you're different now, haven't you seen yourself? Our old clothes barely fit you, you're taller, you've got a bigger chest and have grown to double digits in jeans, your hair is longer and wild, your voice has changed and so has your likes and dislikes. WHAT'S HAPPENED TO YOU…! You talk about schoolwork and the future as if it's right in front of you, waiting for you to take its hand. When you do, will you forget about me? Our times together and the memories within our home…? Where will I be when you catch up with Mr. Future…? Will I be lost in your time and space? Forgotten like an old dollhouse in the corner of the attic…? Guess we will find out when it happens, for now I sit here, in our abandoned apartment.

# 26

## DESTRUCTIVE NORMS

Space and emptiness only for those brave enough to overcome the demand for company, the desire for love, request for life without wonder, without loneliness. Approval and love for oneself for those wise enough to go beyond the boundaries of beauty. The limits of a world's view dissipating for those with the power to see beyond smoky mirrors.

Unity for those willing to look past the darker shade and twisted history. Togetherness for those willing to come together when the world grows apart. Union for those that chose speech, rather than conflict.

In life, many things aid in growing our flames rather than putting them out. But with more people identifying them and contributing to bringing down our 'norms.' We can, as people, live up to the constitution where it states that 'All men are created equal.'

# 27

## LOVING DANGEROUSLY

Love knows no bounds, but when someone loves the other a little too much, you search for those fences you wished you would have put up so long ago. The same thing happened to Alissa Mackintosh. After breaking up with her boyfriend, the two separated. She started to receive messages from him wanting her back and even threatening to kill himself if he wasn't with her. The texts became more violent as the months went by, and that's how we got here.

Alissa's body laid on the ground – motionless, cold. Her hair clumped up in the pool of blood, her neck and wrist bruised. Her ex-boyfriend, Jacob Harris, had broken in and demanded her back. I assume she said no, and he tried to force her. They tussled before he grabbed a blunt object and hit her with it. After a few hours, she woke up in a dark space, with no doors and no windows, only a small beam of light that flew in through the cracks between the poorly-laid bricks. Day in and day out, she'd wake up to food at her feet and she could hear Harris moving around in the house but, with every scream, no one came.

Now with Jacob in custody, after escaping the law for several years, he decides to confess to what he did to Alissa – as to why he kidnapped her and carved 'I will always love you' into her skin.

# 28

## SNOWY EVENING

I continued to walk along what I assumed to be the sidewalk as the snow fell rapidly, trying to enclose me in its stinging cold. The wind grew fierce as I grew closer to home, making it hard to see; and as the cold touched my bare hands, my fingers grew stiff. After a few miles, faint lights glowed in the distance, making the snow a soft yellow and guiding me across my path. I saw houses in the distance, they created smoke in the sky, but the wind blew them away, sending its signal of warmth elsewhere.

I approached one of the windows and peered in, seeing a family gathered around a warm fire and talking about something that wasn't meant for my ears to hear. I frowned a bit, knowing that it's something I couldn't have – comfort amongst my family. Sighing, I walked off, leaving the family to their relaxing evening and allowing the snow to make contact with my face again. Its soft touch gracing my face, creating false tears for the sadness I felt inside.

## 29

## AN INTERESTING WINTER

Something about today seemed to be different, the snow looked whiter and cleaner, like mother nature swept the footsteps away to make the perfect runway for Santa's arrival. As always mom was in the kitchen, singing along with the recording of Michael Bublé on the radio and combining ingredients to make the most divine meal that you've ever tasted. She was there on the holidays so much that she lived there, cooking day in and day out, making the home smell like a bed and breakfast in the morning and the fanciest restaurant at night. If I would walk in, she'd look at me with a smile on her face and a cookie in hand ready to be shoved in my mouth for a confirmed opinion. I loved the way she baked with grace as if she was dancing on ice, it made me happy and put me in the mood to decorate.

    I walked upstairs to the attic and looked around, the corners of the place were a spider's paradise and a bug's nightmare. We never really went up there often, only to make room downstairs and get the decor for any special occasion. I walked in the middle of the room and looked at the door full of supplies, it had boxes waiting to be scooped up and I was ready to collect. As I picked up the box labeled 'Xmas' I investigated the depth of the dark closet, inside was a silhouette of a table and chair with a bulky box on top. I turned on the light and tears swelled in my eyes.

"Daddy?" It was his typewriter; he would sit in the office downstairs and write until his fingers cramped. He loved writing but he made it clear that we were on the top of his list. The typewriter still had the paper in its teeth, with only three words, 'My darling daughter.' It was supposed to be a page just for me, but he never got a chance to finish. I opened the drawer below it and to my surprise, there was a box. It was covered in balloon animals and circus tents, a bright pink bow, and a puffy peanut sticker. I put down the box and picked up the dusty box in the drawer, it was the size of my hand, small but very cute. I scratched the sticker, but it smelled of dust and cobwebs, not the peanut smell I was hoping for. I sat down in his chair and undid the bow carefully as if the box would have turned to dust if I had rushed it. Once the bubblegum-colored bow dropped on the ground, I slowly opened the box, letting the cobwebs that were clinging on the box rip away one by one. What was inside made my heart stop – it was a necklace. It was golden with a small heart charm on the chain and a locket that looked like a gift box. I rubbed my finger on the box until my fingernail unclipped the small latch and burst open the silver object. Inside was a picture of me and my dad in the hospital. This was taken when I was born, me in his arms crying at the top of my lungs but despite the ear-shattering noise he looked at me and smiled, with pure happiness in his eyes and a bundle of joy in his arms.

 I took the necklace and ran downstairs leaving the bulky old box in the darkness of its saddening home. I entered the kitchen in haste and looked at my mother, she faced me with a smile looking at the box in my hand. "What's that baby?" I paused and unboxed the necklace, putting it up to show it to her. She covered her mouth and took it from me, opening it up and looking at me with tears in her eyes. "Where did you get this?" she mumbled, turning it over to see the rest.

"It was in dad's desk… that… that we have upstairs." She nodded and gave it back, looking happy to have seen it but sad to give it away.

"You know that was for your birthday last year, right?" She turned down the radio and sat in front of me in one of the dining chairs. "He wanted to give it to you first thing in the morning so you could show it off at school." She sniffled and wiped her nose as she spoke, her voice horse and shaky. "But… he never even got to." She began to cry looking at the photo in the middle of the table as she sobbed. I looked at her then slowly walked to get the box that I had abandoned upstairs. I knew she wanted to be alone every time she would cry, if I tried to comfort her, she would walk away or say that she was fine. I knew it wasn't true, but it was better than making it worse. After getting the box and decorating the tree I moved to the porch.

The wind outside was whistling, rushing in-between the trees' bare branches and blowing the snow from the roof. Even with a coat, scarf, and gloves, the cold got to me, making my hands stiff and cold to the touch. Once I was finished, I sat on the hanging couch outside and watched cars pass by one by one, sure it was cold, but it was also beautiful. The snow was nature's way of getting into the spirit of the holiday, tree leaves were replaced with snow and roofs' bare tops were dressed in it. For some reason, white looked so amazing on everything, but we decided that green and red were the main colors of the season.

# 30

## WAIT FOR IT...

My heart raced as something approached the door, its small hand jiggling as the monster on the other side begged for a way inside my safe place. As I opened my mouth to speak, crisp air filled my lungs, making my mouth dry and cold.

Again, the doorknob danced frantically in fear, followed by a knock that came from outside, from the unknown. I slunk down into my seat and watched as the door slowly cracked open. I tried to hide as much as the chair would allow but there was no way out of this nightmare.

As the door swung open, I winced at the small whimper the hinges made when slowly closing the door again, but it was too late. The creature was already inside, and it smiled at me. Another step closer, and it shouted with glee, "Time to take your shot, Michelle!"

# 31

## IGNORANCE IS BLISS

It feels like so long ago when someone has ventured into the light, every time they do it seems like they just vanish, but not me or my family. We choose to keep our blindfolds on, we choose to stay in the dark and listen to our rulers, to believe what they say and don't think about the knowledge behind it, just listen like we are supposed to. I remember when me and my friends came back from school, we went to my treehouse and talked about the lessons we were taught in history and how the girls sounded so sweet when talking to us at lunch. As we played 'Guess by Touch' one of my friends had suggested something nobody should be thinking anytime soon. He suggested that we should take off our blindfolds for just one second, to finally see what we all look like or how trees and grass look. While everyone else agreed, I was the only one thinking that this was a very bad idea. I tried to remind them of what happens to people that take off their blindfolds but they didn't want to hear it. After trying to convince me some more, mother had called me for dinner and it was time for them to leave.

After dinner, I cleaned up and went to bed. The thought of knowing what the outside world looked like, what the sweet-sounding girls at my school looked like, or even what I look like lingered in my mind. I couldn't sleep and as I tossed and turned in my bed, I came to a decision; I got up and went to the bathroom and locked the door behind me. I took a deep breath, and I loosened the knot that held my blindfold in place. As I felt my blindfold wiggle a bit, I closed my eyes and let it fall to the bathroom counter; one look I thought as I slowly opened my eyes, but when I did, I jumped back in horror to see what stood, looking back at me. It was a horrid creature, his skin barely clinging to its body and bone revealing itself. I touched my face to see the creature doing the same. I held back a scream as I realized what that horrid creature was, that horrid creature that made me want to look away and vomit was me. I quickly put my blindfold back on and scurried to bed. The rulers were right, ignorance is bliss.

# 32

## UNHEALTHY RELATIONSHIP

We build empires together. We grow communities together, we house religions together, and we make a legacy together. But we can't be together if we have to fight for equality, if we have to make ourselves known and correct your grammar when you say "I" instead of "We." We made America what it is. We made this place stand out, and we can continue to do so if you give us the respect and the love that we deserve. Only then can we be together again. Only then can there be growth and change.

# 33

## FOR THE THEATER

You're poison and you comprehend that, your words are like the vines of a maneater and your embrace is like tar. But yet I am here, being some type of cane for your injured self-esteem, being a defibrillator for your dying will to go on. I stay because I feel like your fragile ego could never stay together without me. However, we know that's not true. You're loud, proud, and you know how to control. After I walked into your life, you became a beggar, and I gave you the coins you already had in the back of your pocket. Day in and day out, you play this game that only so many times I can lose. The moment I start winning, you become hurt. You became this broken-faced doll that shows a different, darker face than the one you put on for me and the masses.

Some may choose to put your false pieces back together when they start winning, but I won't. I intend to win, and if that makes you shiver and cower in fear, then so be it. Because two faces are only for the theater, and it's about time that the curtains close on yours.

## 34

## SOMEWHERE IN THE BLOOD

It was pouring outside, no one around for miles and broken streetlights didn't make this adventure any better. The school's windows were black letting us know that no one was home which was good for us in our case. "Can we hurry up? The rain ain't stopping no time soon," Angel said in a hushed tone, she was holding herself as we walked, obviously regretting her decision to only wear a sweater. I laughed and stopped at the school doors opening them with ease.

"After you, my lady," I said, smiling at her as she walked in mumbling something under her breath. It was so different at night, colder because the heat was off, darker and definitely creepy. I looked around a bit before taking out my flashlight.

"Are you sure this is necessary?" Angel looked at me, her hair clung to her face desperately for warmth as she took off her hood and dropped her bag down on the floor.

"Yeah, let's just make a mess and get out okay, no big whoop." I walked toward the desk in the middle of the room and sat in the chair. "Go check out the place, I'll meet you in the office in a few," I said as I began to pull draws.

Everything was nicely packed in Mrs. Marshall's desk, so it was only right to destroy that order. As I rummaged through her things, a folder appeared amongst all the magazines and the banana-flavored Laffey Taffy – it was red, marked 'IMPORTANT' in all caps. "Might as well take a peek." I opened up the folder, it was filled with late sign-in sheets for the week and a sticky note with a password and username. I smiled and opened up the computer on the desk, typing in the information and as expected the computer opened up to me exposing an open tab of blackjack and a web search for handbags.

"Stupid Chris, can't you just be a normal kid?" Angel mumbled as she walked into the main office; it was quiet, full of desks, a printer, and a coffee machine. She grabbed the keys off the wall and walked out to the hall searching for one of the worst teacher's rooms of all, Mr. Smith. He knew how to get under everyone's skin and since she was here, she might as well get under his. The door read 'History room 209' on the door and with no effort Angel slid the key into place and unlocked the door, her nose was met with a foul odor as usual but, in this case, it wasn't Mr. Smith's lack of deodorant. She looked around until she found his desk all the way in the upper left corner. She ran to it and opened up his drawers, taking them out and emptying them completely. When she was done, she spotted his locked closet; it was always locked with chains preventing anyone from going in. The closet was never open and had a terrible smell like something had died inside. It had always creeped her out but if it was that heavily guarded, then she had to know what was in there and why.

 Angel screamed again at the sight; it was Cassy's body in there. Her lips sewed together like two pieces of fabric and her body nude, there was so much blood and knife marks I was surprised that you kept together so well. I wanted to scream but fear filled my lungs, refusing to let me breathe. After a while the smell got to me, dry blood and a rotting body don't mix well and made me want to vomit. As I looked at Cassy closer, her eyes twitched and her fingers began to move. She opened her eyes and screamed, holding her arms out for help while grabbing me in the process.

I woke up, sweat rushing out of me in waves and my heart running circles inside of my chest. I checked the time on my alarm clock, it was 2.34 in the morning and it was still pitch-black outside. I looked around my room hoping that someone was there to calm me down but there was no one. I'd been having these dreams for a month now and going into that class every sixth period wasn't helping my case. It came to a point where Angel and I would flinch every time Mr. Smith called on us to answer, voices shaking vigorously with fear hoping that he'd move on.

We have no idea what happened after week three because after that the smell was gone and the closet was free of its chains, but Mr. Smith still found himself in front of the classroom, teaching regularly, as if nothing was ever in there. Some think it's just the janitor actually getting to his job, but we know what we saw and my mind ain't planning on forgetting it. It was the last day of winter break, I had forgotten to get any work done and since I was up I might as well start. I opened up my history book, flipping through pages searching for a clean one but all I got were drawings after drawings. They were all of her, her body bloody and shredded, her neck bruised and swollen, her lips sewn and faded, and her hair matted and limp. It terrified me to see them, but it was what I saw, when mom asked me that night why I came home so late I couldn't truly answer so I made up a lie, only to have her flash into my head.

*I can't sleep*, Angel thought as she tossed and turned. It has been a month since she had been in front of that poor girl's body, but it only felt like yesterday. She looked at her closet, half scared of what she might find and also half worried of what might be hiding behind her coats and jackets. It hasn't been the same since, class in history is a terrifying eternity, dreams have now become nightmarish and closets look unapproachable. "What did happen to her though and why?" Angel says out loud, but no one answers. She turns toward the window, pondering about… her, about Cassy.

It was noisy in the lunchroom as always and the smell of today's lunch lingered in the halls; it was time to eat and ain't nobody was trying to eat last. As I sat down at my table all alone, I watched News 12, the only thing ever on the big television hoisted up in the middle of the cafeteria. It was boring but still I was interested, wondering what was happening around the world.

"Can I sit here?" Angel said with a smile on her face. I nodded absently, eyes glued to the screen as they talked about a shooting in Queens. She sat down and talked about her day so far, not really concerned about my interest. "Anyway, I said that she sho—oh my God!" Angel looked at the screen in horror, it was Cassy; they had found her body in a dumpster three miles from here. They talked about her being missing for five weeks and that some old man looking for plastics had found her.

"How could someone do that?" someone said not far from us; we looked at each other knowing that Mr. Smith might have known someone went into his closet and saw her, so he had to think fast and get rid of the body.

After lunch was a blur, I went through the rest of my day stuck in my head. I thought about what they had said on the news about it being a brutal murder. I knew that once they'd labeled it as such, they weren't going to look into it any further. I saw Mr. Smith's face when two girls were talking about it. He looked relaxed, not worried, just normal, making me sick.

*Why would he do that?* Angel thought, she was kind as far as she knew, she never harmed anyone and was a grade A student. If Mr. Smith didn't do it; he was still guilty for keeping her body in that awful closet. As she let her mind spiral, a note was passed on her desk.

It read 'Library after school 5.24.' Chris looked at her, his face full of concern and determination; just like her, he wanted to know, he wanted to know who killed Cassy.

After school we raced to the library to get checked on one of their computers, hoping to look up more information on Cassy's case. We stayed until the last second looking but all we found was the exact information that was said on the news.

"Maybe they will update it...? It just aired today," Angel said, trying to calm me down.

"NO!" I screamed. "We are going to go back to school tonight, if there's a body there's got to be some form of explanation on a paper or something in that hellhole!" With that it was decided, tonight we pack, to go to a place filled with dread in the dead of night; tonight, we're going back to school.

As we arrived at the school, it was locked. I guess they decided to lock it when we went in and messed up the place, so we looked for another way in. It was dark in the back of the school, but the lunchroom door was still unlocked. We sneaked in and looked around; it was dark, and the lunch tables were standing up against the walls, the smell of lunch was still inside but it was faint and a little stale if you could even smell that. "Go check the office for the keys, I'll check the file room," Angel said as she turned on her flashlight. I nodded as I headed upstairs.

Angel hated the basement, but it was better than going back into that room, she descended slowly, making sure that her foot touched every step. It was dark and the air was hot and moist, it didn't help that the stairs spiraled down, making the monsters around her have an advantage to get her around each and every corner. When she reached the door, she pushed it open, the door moaning with all its might. There were a ton of filing cabinets in rows, all dusty and housing the most terrifying creatures yet. She sighed. "Let's get searching."

I was angry. "All these damn keys for WHAT!" I screamed as I tried to cram the keys into the office door. It was stupid to have all these keys that go to the classrooms and not a separate one for the office itself. When I finally scored the right key, I opened the door. Mr. Cameron's room was cold but tidy, the desk had separate piles of work from bills to plans for future trips. I don't want to blame this guy for a murder! He's cool, I come talk to him every now and again about boxing and girl advice, but I don't want to see him get arrested! I sighed and went into his drawers. There were folders upon folders but, nevertheless, they didn't stand out. I gave up after a full three-sixty search and got on to his computer; I lifted up the glass cat and took the small yellow slip out from under it. I unfolded it and typed in his username and password; when his computer allowed me access, I saw only one folder. It read important in bold and red, and my stomach turned. "Please don't be a part of all this, Mr. Cameron, I don't even want to think about you killing someone. Let alone hiding the body." I opened it, and there it was.

The filing cabinets were all filled with nothing of any importance, just graduated classes, old trip plans and construction on the school. Angel didn't see any point in looking anymore but something told her to keep looking just for a while longer. As she closed the cabinet, another opened slightly; she looked at it, puzzled and walked toward it with wonder and a little bit of fear.

 She opened it wider – just more boring files – but when she looked closer, she realized the folders read 'Cassy' on all the tabs, she swallowed but her fear closed her throat tight. She picked one up and opened it. "No, no, no, no…" It was what she was looking for all right, but part of her wished she didn't.

Leaving was easier than getting in, we met up in the lunchroom and ran back to my place to look at the documents more clearly. We sat on my bed with the lights on and the window opened a crack, every page full of her living life, what she liked to do and where she was all day in school. She was a 10th grader, had outstanding grades, 5'4" and had dark brown hair; she took trips to the library a lot during lunch but after February she hung out in Mr. Smith's room. "What if they had... you know... a thing going on?" Angel asked with disgust in her voice and curiosity in her eyes.

"Maybe, we can't know for sure if that even happened... I mean look at these papers, they're full of information but not the information that we were looking for," I said as I rolled my eyes and laid back on my bed. "We'll figure it out, just hold on." Angel got up and picked up the papers.

"I'll go and look at these more at home, mom's blowing up my phone," she said as she packed up and went out the door, yelled out a good night and I watched her leave for home from my window. I sighed again and stared at the ceiling, listening to the wind whistling in my ear as I drifted off to sleep.

*It's surprisingly dark outside for only 9.00 at night*, Angel thought as she walked home; it was too late to go back to Chris's house now and if she did her mom would be pissed for the late notice so she pressed on. The wind howled as the cars raced passed, making her hair dance excitedly. *Mmmmm-Mmmmm*, Angel's phone vibrated in her pocket as she was halfway home. Angel checked her phone, '*Whatever you're looking for, stop – you might find something that you won't not want to discover.*' She stared at her phone; it was from an unknown number. For some reason it knew what Angel and Chris were up to and it didn't like it. *Mmmmmm-Mmmmm,* another text popped up. '*Throw the papers in the trash on the left around the corner, you don't need the info in there, it's pointless. If you don't, think and consider how I know where you are.*' Angel jumped back and looked around; there wasn't a soul in sight but afraid of who might be sending these she took off her bag, gathered the papers in her hands, and as the stranger had said, threw them away and continued walking.

As Angel reached home and looked around one last time before getting her keys and unlocking the door, she went in expecting her mother to be waiting, speech in mind, ready to let loose on her. But to Angel's surprise, no one was home, only her and the moonlight that was coming in from the windows. *Mmmmm-Mmmmmm.* Angel's phone vibrated again, '*Good girl, now go to bed, you have a big day tomorrow… See you at school.*' Angel dropped her phone in horror and ran upstairs, whoever was texting her knew who she was and that… could be a major issue.

"You seem on edge all of a sudden," Chris pointed out as we walked the halls.

"No, I'm fine I'm just on the lookout for suspects," Angel said as she looked around, she didn't sleep last night, but how could she? If someone knew her number and where she was going, there's no telling if they were right in the next room as she tossed and turned all night. She looked at her phone, afraid to receive another text telling her that she'd be late for gym or that she had forgotten something in Ms. Koi's room. Chris had asked for the documents in the morning at breakfast, looking into Angel's eyes with worry when she had told him she didn't have it. "I threw it out last night, as I told you before, we didn't need it. It was just some information on how she spent her time, not how she died or who she meddled with."

With that Chris settled down a little, sighing with somewhat of a relief in his voice, "Good, I guess that's one less thing to worry about."

I was nervous, breaking into a room in broad daylight, sure, in the middle of the night is risky but in the MORNING...! Geez, what have we gotten into this year? I chuckled to myself as I picked the lock to Mr. Lerner's room. He was in the teacher's lounge yacking it up with Ms. Jefferson and Mr. Davis as they ate their lunch and graded papers. As Angel watched the halls for any unsuspecting human, I unlocked the door and made my way in. Mr. Lerner's room was cold for a room on the top floor, no windows were opened and the curtains he had brought from home were drawn, leaving the sunlight on the bench as I made it up to the stands. His bookcase was riddled with old books I've read so many times. If I had randomly picked one from its humble home, I'd be able to tell you what it was about as if I had written it myself. "Enough stargazing already," Angel had hissed from the hallway. I nodded and went to his desk that had sat in the middle of the room. It was neat, with piles of graded work to worksheets for his next lesson. I dabbled in his folders as I tried to keep things the way he had left them, moving around his things and opening drawers here and there for a thorough search. As I made it to my last draw, I heard heavy, swift footsteps approaching the room. "Hi, Mr. Lerner, how's everything?" Angel yelled toward the footsteps, but they didn't stop as they mumbled a hello.

I began to panic as he came closer, I looked around, hoping for an easy escape. As I saw it, I darted toward the closet, opening it swiftly and closing it behind me as he arrived. "Where did I put it?" he mumbled, searching his desk as he checked his phone now and again.

"Did you find it?" A voice whispered from behind him. He turned.

"N-n-no," he stuttered to the man.

"Listen here, bud," the man said as he grabbed his shirt, lifting him from where he stood. "Find me those documents or you'll be rotting in a closet next!" He hissed as he threw him down to the floor. Mr. Lerner nodded frantically as he laid there, looking paler than ever and like a scared child as the man loomed over him. "Good no—" He stopped as I covered my mouth. "What was that?" he said as he looked around, slowly stopping at the closet.

"Oh dip," I whispered. "Crap, crap, crap," I whispered as the large man came closer, his fist was clenched and he grinded his teeth as if he was going to stuff me into a teddy bear skin after he beat me to death. I backed up as far as the closet would allow before I shut my eyes and began to pray for my untimely death.

"Oh, here I have it!" Mr. Lerner said proudly with a hint of fear in his voice.

The man calmed a bit as he turned toward him. "That's amazing, Jeremy…! And here I thought I had to nail you to the ceiling." His laugh was rather sinister for his own joke, but Mr. Lerner didn't laugh, he only got paler because of it.

"Right-o… So, here you go." He handed the man a flash drive and some paperwork while forcing a smile and hiding the sudden flinch when the man grabbed it.

Angel paced around in the hallway as she waited for Chris. "Come on, don't tell me they caught you," she mumbled as she bit her nails in worry and frustration. As she paced some more, she heard the door slam, she looked up. "Oh no." She raced to the bathroom and closed the door, laying down on the dirty, cold floor and watching from the vent on the door, she saw Mr. Lerner and the blond-haired man shake hands before he walked off out of sight. Angel was confused but a little more relaxed that Chris was nowhere to be seen. When Mr. Lerner had vanished back to the teacher's lounge Angel had run to his door and knocked. "Hey, dumb-dumb, are you there?" She put her ear to the door, hoping for a response.

"Yeah, yeah, I'm here," I said as I crawled out of the closet, wiping off my clothes and walking around the room again.
"Mr. Lerner had given that guy a flash drive and some paperwork," Angel shouted. I opened the door, making Angel lose her balance and almost fall.
"Really... Dammit, I could have got that, but that guy would have killed him if I had," I said to myself almost in a whisper, I made my way to his desk again, searching more than ever to see if I had missed something like before.
Angel watched as Chris messed up Mr. Lerner's desk. "Have you seen that guy around here before, like as a janitor or a sub... a part of the lunch staff maybe?"
She looked at the window as Chris responded with a senseless mumble of "I don't know." As he continued his search. Angel sighed and checked the closet, moving every

jacket and checking every pocket for something.

"Ah-ha!" Angel said with excitement as she pulled out a flash drive from Mr. Lerner's raincoat.

I stopped my search to look at the treasure that Angel had found. "That's amazing!" I cheered as I took it from her and placed it in my sweater pocket, zipping it up and patting it. "Let's go to the library after school to check it out." Angel nods as we hear the bell and head out the door to the next class, almost skipping in joy.

Mr. Lerner came back to his room after the children had left, somewhat perplexed as to how his door was open after he closed it. "Mm..." He grunted as he made his way inside, seeing his classroom as if a tornado had passed through. "I know I left the desk a mess, but not that badly." He picked up the papers and fixed it up as he saw his closet wide open, his face turning as pale as the moon as he walked toward it, seeing everything out of place and his raincoat robbed. "Dammit!" Mr. Lerner screamed as he panicked, he looked at the floor of the closet, seeing that someone had made a pathway in all the dust. "Hmmm... Someone was in the closet earlier," he mumbled as he closed the closet.

He went to his desk and picked up the phone, dialing a number and fiddling with his shirt button. "Yes, hello," he said urgently. "We have a problem... It's about code A... Someone knows."

As Chris and Angel walked toward the library after school, they could feel a chill in the air. Some may have said it was just the fall, crisp air that swirled overhead, bringing the warm-colored leaves with it. But they knew well that it was the anxiety of the trip that made the world so much colder.

"Should we get something to eat before we... you know?" Angel said as she stuffed her hands in her pockets and shrunk into her jacket.

"No, too jumpy to eat, let's just get in, plug in, and get the hell out and to a safe place," I said as I held the door open and let Angel glide through before closing the door behind me. I huffed. "Good afternoon, Ms. Jason!" I said in a rather cheery voice, making Angel flinch.

"Oh, good afternoon, Chris, how nice to see you!" She quickly glanced at Angel. "Who's your friend?"

"Oh, this is Angel." Angel gave a shy smile and a little wave before putting her hands back in their rightful place.

"Ah, well hello, Angel, what can I help you with today? A book on history, comics, magazines?" Ms. Jason smiled as the room got silent as if everyone wanted to hear what we came for.

I turned a little pale and leaned in, whispering, "Can... Can we go to the back? We've got a history project, and we need to look over some documents."

"Oh, of course, dear." She slid a small key toward me as she stamped a small paper and gave it to me as well. "You have a good hour before the Fabian brothers come in for their daily meeting," Ms. Jason said as she turned herself back to her computer, typing away, and returning the room to its whispers and hidden secrets.

"Let's go," I say as I grab Angel's arm and lead her behind all the bookshelves and to a rusted door that reads 'Quiet Room' in broken, faded, black letters.

Angel cleared her throat as Chris pushed open the whiny door and sat in front of a computer, the only thing that looked new out of everything in this dark room. "Mm... I hope you don't expect me to sit down, this place hasn't been dusted probably since the 1900s," she said as she closed the door.

"That's fine," Chris said as he started up the computer and typed something in while squinting at the small paper. Angel sighed and stood behind him as he plugged in the flash drive and started up the projector. "Click on it..."

"Yeah, yeah, hold your—oh God." I clicked on the flash drive labeled 'Security files' and opened it up.

"Security camera footage 1-20-17, Security camera footage 1-21-17... S-security camera footage 1-22-17," Angel read as she covered her mouth.

"Why would Mr. Lerner have this?" I said, turning toward her. "WHY WOULD HE HAVE THIS?"

"I don't know... I don't know," she stammered as I clicked on the first file commanding a video to pop up, waiting to start...

We hunkered in taciturnity as the play button anticipated our decision. "Press it; we have to know whether it's the information we're looking for," Angel said as her nails burrowed into my shoulder, but I couldn't feel the pain, only my heart hammering like a drum and my breathing quickening. Slowly but surely, I played the video, it began with kids strolling into class and taking their seats; we didn't know any of them but one, and when I noticed her my heart froze. It was Cassy and she looked lively, the camera was propped up on what appeared to be the whiteboard and everyone's face came into view. She looked like her newer self, but her lips were full and bright red, her cheeks flushed with pink, and her eyes a beautiful almond brown. She was clean of any markings on her soft skin and her hair added volume to the point that it made her shoulders disappear under the sea of locks. I smirked a bit, quickly dropping into the chair so Angel couldn't see my admiration for such a girl, if she'd be alive now, she would be in eleventh and I would be close behind, wishing that I could hear her gentle song directed at me.

After some time of studying the records, an hour had passed, and the twins came to collect their meeting space. As we walked back to Angel's place to talk more clandestinely about what we observed, I couldn't get Cassy out of my head; her beauty and her intelligence in class made her seem like a siren under the waves and I was her unknowing pirate, sailing in the unforgiving sea. Hopefully, we can bring justice to her death, but until then I'll keep the flash drive close, and Cassy closer.

After stealing from Mr. Lerner, he disappeared, nobody saw him or heard from him for days. On the loudspeaker, they were saying he got sick, and we should wish him the best, but Angel and I knew that he was probably locked up in his house or got fired for letting crucial information slip away from him so easily. We also started to see security marching around the school, which made our plans to sneak in that week a no-go.

Nothing much went on after that, just school and exams. I did start going to the library more. I can't help but replay the videos of my sweet Cassy on the projector in the back room. Something about her made me addicted, maybe her gentle voice or her lovely locks that bounce on her shoulders when she walks into the classroom every day. Even though there wasn't anything monumental on the tapes, it was still amazing to see what could have been.

After school, Angel walked home on her own, again. It was evident that Chris didn't really care much for her any more and just started to slip away. She sighed and continued walking home, checking her phone now and again, hoping Chris would at least call her to explain. But instead of him, it was the unknown number. Angel stopped and looked in horror at the message. It was a picture of her, on her phone, that very moment, she looked around frantically. "Who's out there?" she screamed out into the empty street. She became paranoid, thinking that one day she would come into contact with the stalker, and have to choose between interaction or running away like a scared child from a mascot at Disney world.

As nighttime approached Angel rocked herself to sleep in her room; her mother was out working again, leaving her only child alone and unarmed for when the monsters of the night would be brave enough to confront her. She stared at the photo of her, trying to see if, in the picture, was some clue as to who her stalker was, but no luck. She sat up slowly and thought a bit before texting, '*Where are you now? And what do you want?*' She hoped to get some information if they were taking time out of their day to stalk her. In no time, they texted back.

'*Outside your house, I just want to play a game.*'

Angel paused, re-examining the text again and again as she struggled to stay composed. The stalker was outside her house, and her mom wasn't home. Neither was she going to jeopardize her already-compromised safety by investigating. She breathed in strongly then began typing,

'*What game are we going to play?*' It took a while before recognizing that she had been holding her breath.

Before long, bubbles popped up, and so did a reply, '*Something like twenty questions, if you will.*'

A hiatus, then another text, '*Give information, take information for your troubles.*'

Angel was puzzled that they would play a game like this; previously, they wanted the evidence gone, now they wished to assist? Something wasn't right here, so she formulated her question carefully before typing a response. '*Why do you want to help me now?*'

After some time had passed, her phone buzzed. '*Because I happen to like where this is going, and without extra, credible information, there is no entertainment.*'

Angel huffed, she disliked knowing that someone obtained some satisfaction in her absurd world, but she pressed on. '*Did Cassy have any connections with the teachers?*'

Another buzz. '*No, she kept to herself, but people loved to chase after her, some would say she put a spell on anyone who saw her.*'

She rolled her eyes. "Nobody is that pretty, come on," she muttered. '*Why did she die?*'

She heard a muffled giggle from outside. It made her stiff as another text appeared, '*I can't tell you that, you're going to have to go hunting.*'

'*What can you tell me?*'

'*You're on the right track, just might have to get a little personal with the breaking in.*'

She knew what they meant by that and sighed. '*Oops, time's up.*'

'*Wait, I didn't even ask all twenty questions, and you never got your information.*' Footsteps faded outside as one last text appeared.

'*Oh, I already have all my information, honey, plus you're asking too many of the right questions, bye now. I hope to be entertained.*' And with that, they were gone, and Angel was blocked from ever sending to them again, her only form of information, gone with the wind.

After some time, Angel finally dared to ask Chris if he wanted to do something dangerous, and before she could finish, he had sprung up from his lawn chair and threw his fists in the air. "Hell yeah!" he said in enthusiasm as he rushed inside to get his equipment. But what he didn't know was how risky the assignment would be.

When I came back outside, I followed Angel to a strange house. It wasn't abandoned clearly. The shutters were shut, but the lawn was clean and freshly mowed. I chuckled a bit, "What are we going to do here? Ding dong ditch? Because if so I ju—"

But before I could finish, Angel pressed her finger against my lip and told me to 'Pipe down.' As a man in regular attire with a briefcase walked out and to his car.

I looked at him, then became suddenly alarmed when I saw it was Mr. Smith getting ready to head to work for Saturday school. "Woah, woah, woah," I whispered, "what the hell are we doing here?"

"We're going to break in," she hissed back as Mr. Smith started his car and drove off, allowing his music to play him out.

"W-what? What is with you, Angel?"

"You said we should find out what happened, right? So, we're going to. Now come on." She ran over to the house and opened the gate, bruising the poor grass under it as she walked up to the door and began picking at the lock with a bobby pin. I waited nervously behind her, continuously checking if anyone was watching us. Something about Angel's attitude and determination bothered me. Maybe I was just tired or caught off guard. Before I could finish my thought, she opened the door. Walked inside and immediately went through the little credenza that waited for your belongings. I sighed and started looking too.

It wasn't long before we stumbled upon Smith's office and found some evidence, what to do with it we didn't really know. Angel gathered it in her bag as Chris fixed everything to make it look like nobody was home. She rolled her eyes as she walked out. *Buzz, Buzz*. Her phone went off once again, it was a different number this time, but all the same chills. '*Good job, hope to see more of what happens next. Keep me posted ;)*'

Angel stuffed her phone in her pocket and waited for Chris at the door. "Tomorrow will be hell," she mumbled as she locked the door and went her separate way back home.

# 35

## NEXT TIME, I PROMISE

I lay on my bed next to the window, the rays of the sun pressing against it; somehow getting in without the slightest clue of when it will be dragged back out, leaving the world in a temporary darkness. I stay, staring at the ceiling, hoping to feel the sun on my skin and see it dancing in the sky. But every day is a new excuse only to be followed by, 'Next time.' Sometimes, though, the doors do open, and I can run through the grass in the yard and touch a daisy's silk with my fingers. Other times I'm locked away hoping for another sunny day, but instead I'm met with an endless winter. Its cold hands clutching the windows, leaving splinters of ice at its hinges. Its breath creeping through the cracks of the floorboards, grabbing at my feet and making them numb to the pain. And every winter I turn on the heaters, the fireplace and even some candles to light up this abandoned space. But yet I still feel the cold reaching my heart, freezing it over as the hope for a better day grows weak. I still feel the loneliness and the cold biting at my nose. Maybe one day I'll see the sun, maybe one day the clouds won't be so gray, and maybe someday the tears of the melting snow will be no more. But maybe next time, "I promise."